W9-ASE-714

New Friends, True Friends, Stuck-Like-Glue Friends

by Virginia Kroll

Illustrated by Rose Rosely

WM. B. EERDMANS PUBLISHING COMPANY
Grand Rapids, Michigan

255 Jefferson Ave. S.E., Grand Rapids, Michigan 49503

Printed in Singapore

00 99 98 97 96 95 94 10 9 8 7 6 5 4 3 2 1

Library of Congress Cataloging-in-Publication Data

Kroll, Virginia L.
New friends, true friends, stuck-like-glue friends / by Virginia Kroll;
illustrated by Rose Rosely.
p. cm.
Summary: Illustrations and rhyming text provide a look at
all kinds of friendships.
ISBN 0-8028-5085-5
[1. Friendship – Fiction. 2. Stories in rhyme.]
I. Rosely, Rose, 1961– ill. II. Title.
PZ8.3.K8997Ne 1994
[E] – dc20 94-27557
CIP
AC

Book design by Joy Chu

For Jim Landau, my new friend,
Grace Meyers, my true friend, and
Katherine Smith, my stuck-like-glue friend

V.L.K.

To Hulo Moon and our cosmic family

R. R.

Small friends

Tall friends

Playing-soccerball friends

Talk friends
Chalk friends
Come-and-take-a-walk friends

Wriggly friends
Squiggly friends
Laughing and giggly friends

104
SHOW AND TELL
Science

Riding friends
Gliding friends

Seeking-and-hiding friends

Bumble friends
Humble friends

Toss, turn, and tumble friends

Eating friends
Treating friends
Calling-a-meeting friends

Glad friends

Sad friends

Please-don't-be-mad friends

School friends
Jewel friends
Lounging-by-the-pool friends

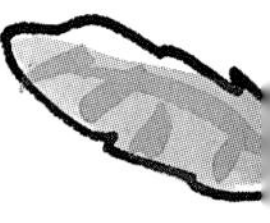

Witty friends
Kitty friends
Living-in-the-city friends

Joy friends
Toy friends
Singing girl-and-boy friends

Light friends
Bright friends
Glow-white-at-night friends

Bug friends

Snug friends

Sharing-a-warm-hug friends

Young friends
Old friends
Hot friends
Cold friends

All-kinds-of-weather friends

Always-together friends!